W9-AZV-017

Cow
in the Dark

For Hectorin and Rebeca

Cow in the Dark

New Kids Media™ is published by Baker Book House Company, P.O. Box 6287, Grand Rapids, MI 49516-6287

ISBN 0-8010-4476-6

Printed in the Indonesia

1 2 3 4 5 6 7 – 03 02 01 00

Todd Aaron Smith

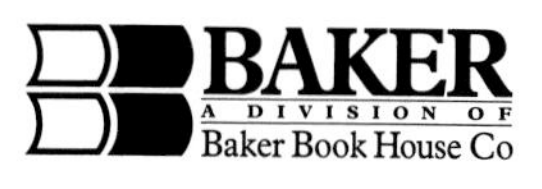

It was a very dark night, and Cow could not sleep. A storm was approaching, and the wind was whistling and blowing things around outside.

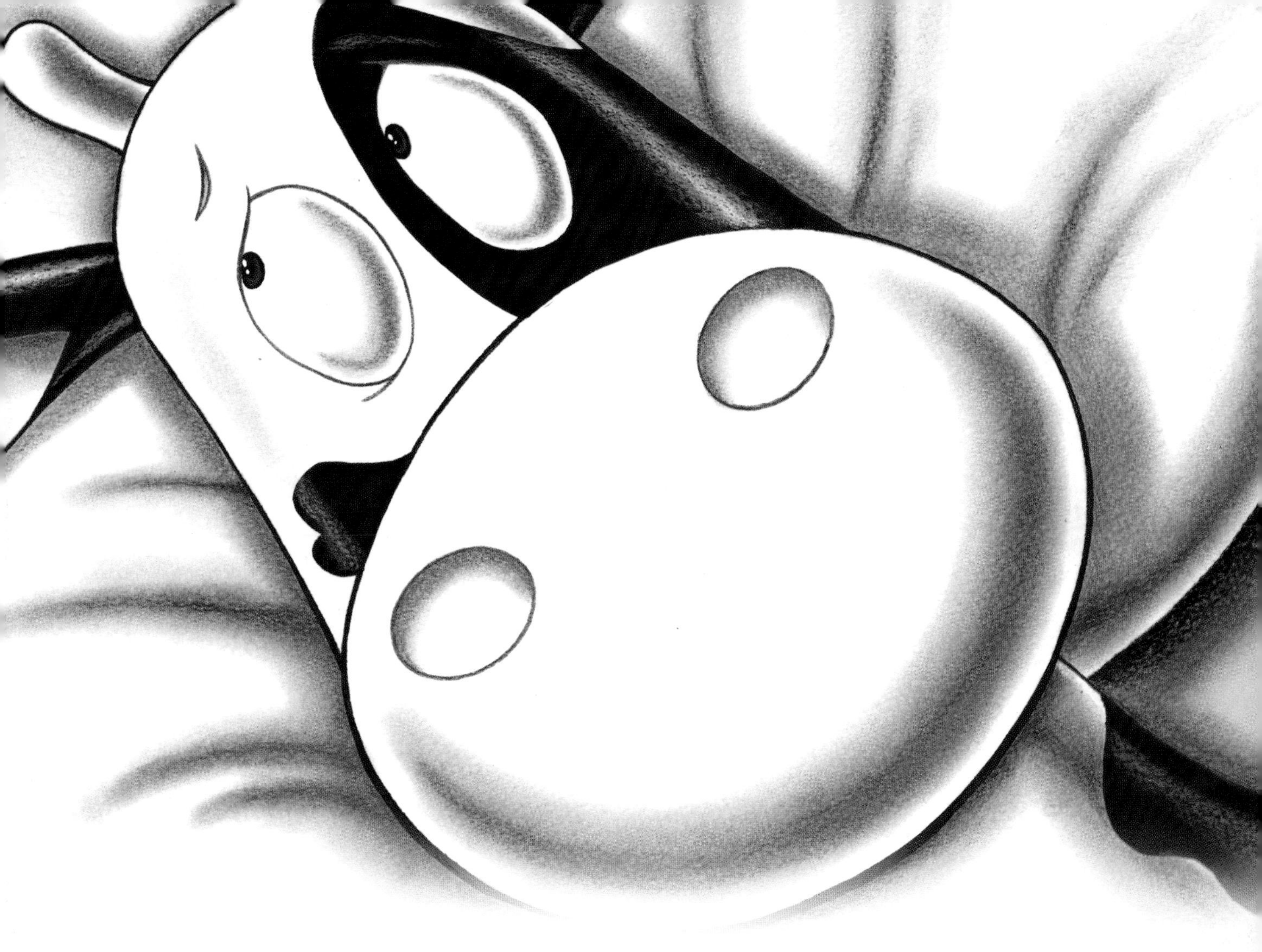

Cow could hear those noises out in the darkness–
noises that she did not remember hearing before. Cow was becoming frightened.

After a while, Cow decided to wake up her friend Pig. She told Pig that she could hear noises out in the darkness. "I think there's something out there," said Cow.

"WHAT?! Oh, NO!" Pig jumped up! "You stay here, Cow! I'll go and get Horse! Maybe he'll know what to do!"

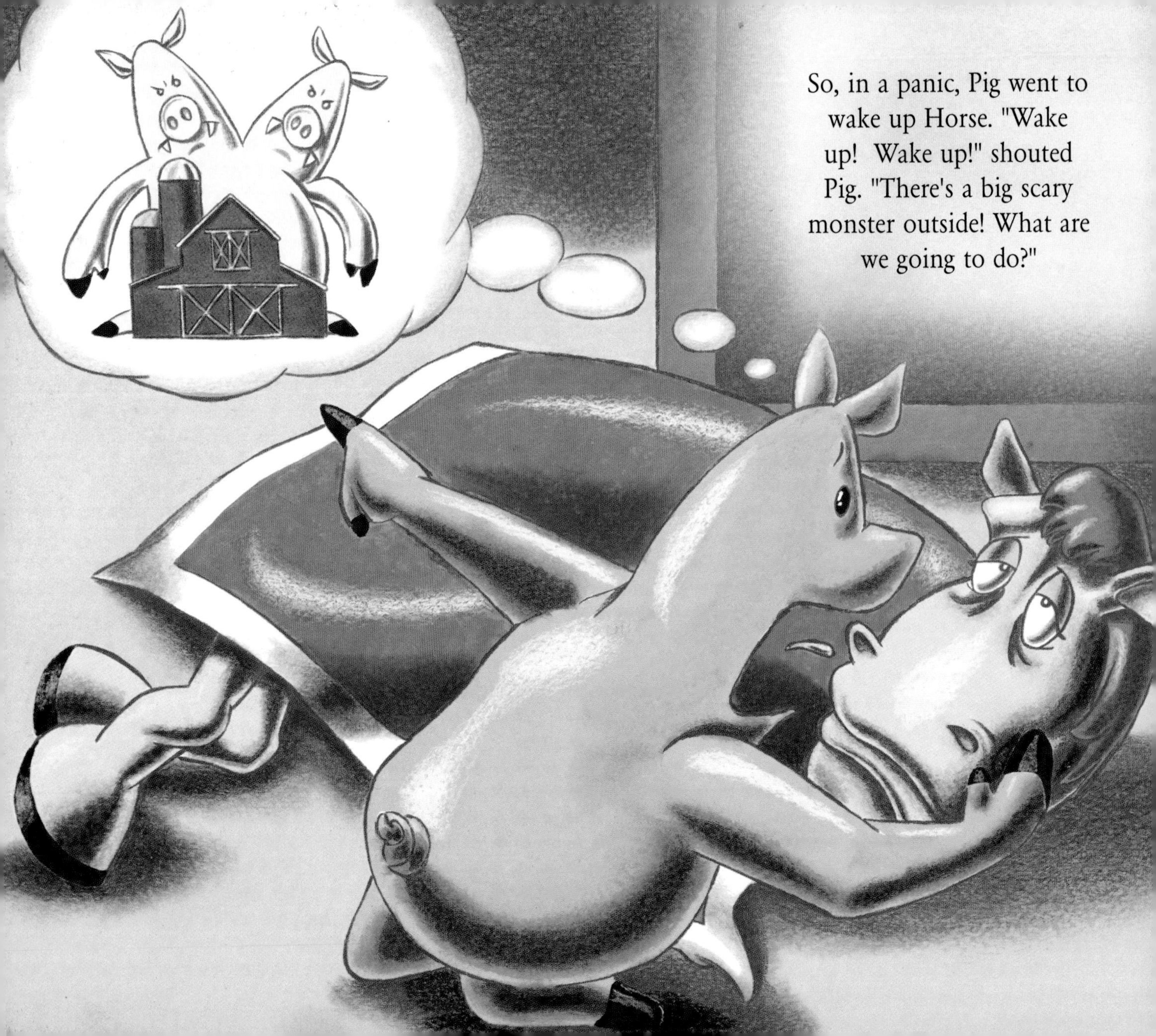

So, in a panic, Pig went to wake up Horse. "Wake up! Wake up!" shouted Pig. "There's a big scary monster outside! What are we going to do?"

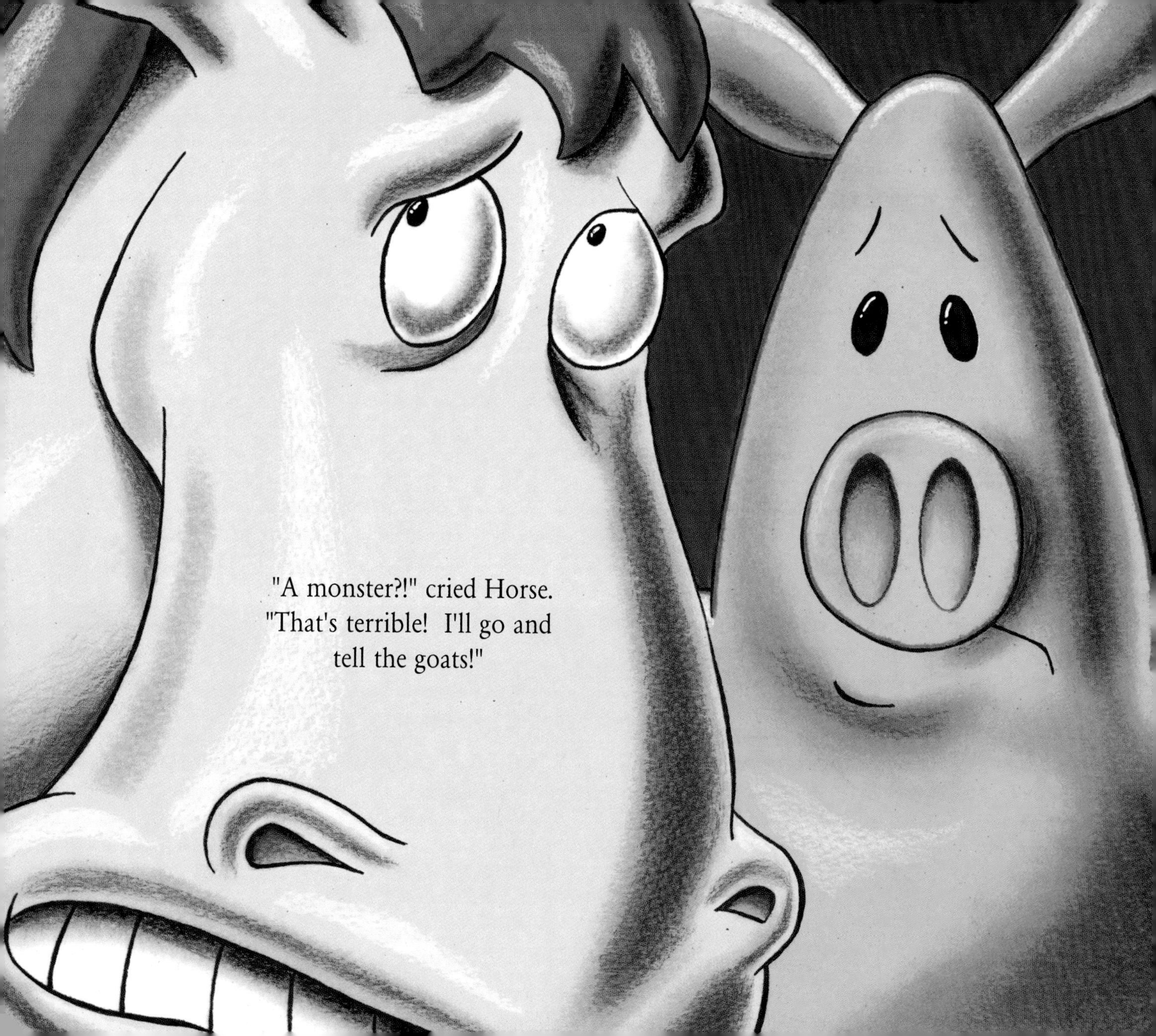

"A monster?!" cried Horse.
"That's terrible! I'll go and
tell the goats!"

So Horse woke up some goats. "Help!" said Horse. "There are three big green monsters outside the barn door!"

"EEEEK!" said the goats. "What do we do?!"
"I don't know!" Pig said. "I thought you would know what to do!"
"Let's go tell everyone!"

So that's what they did. They woke up all of the animals, one by one, in a panic. "There are seventeen angry gigantic monsters outside about to come in!"

This news, of course, caused complete pandemonium with the animals. As the story was passed along, it grew bigger and bigger!

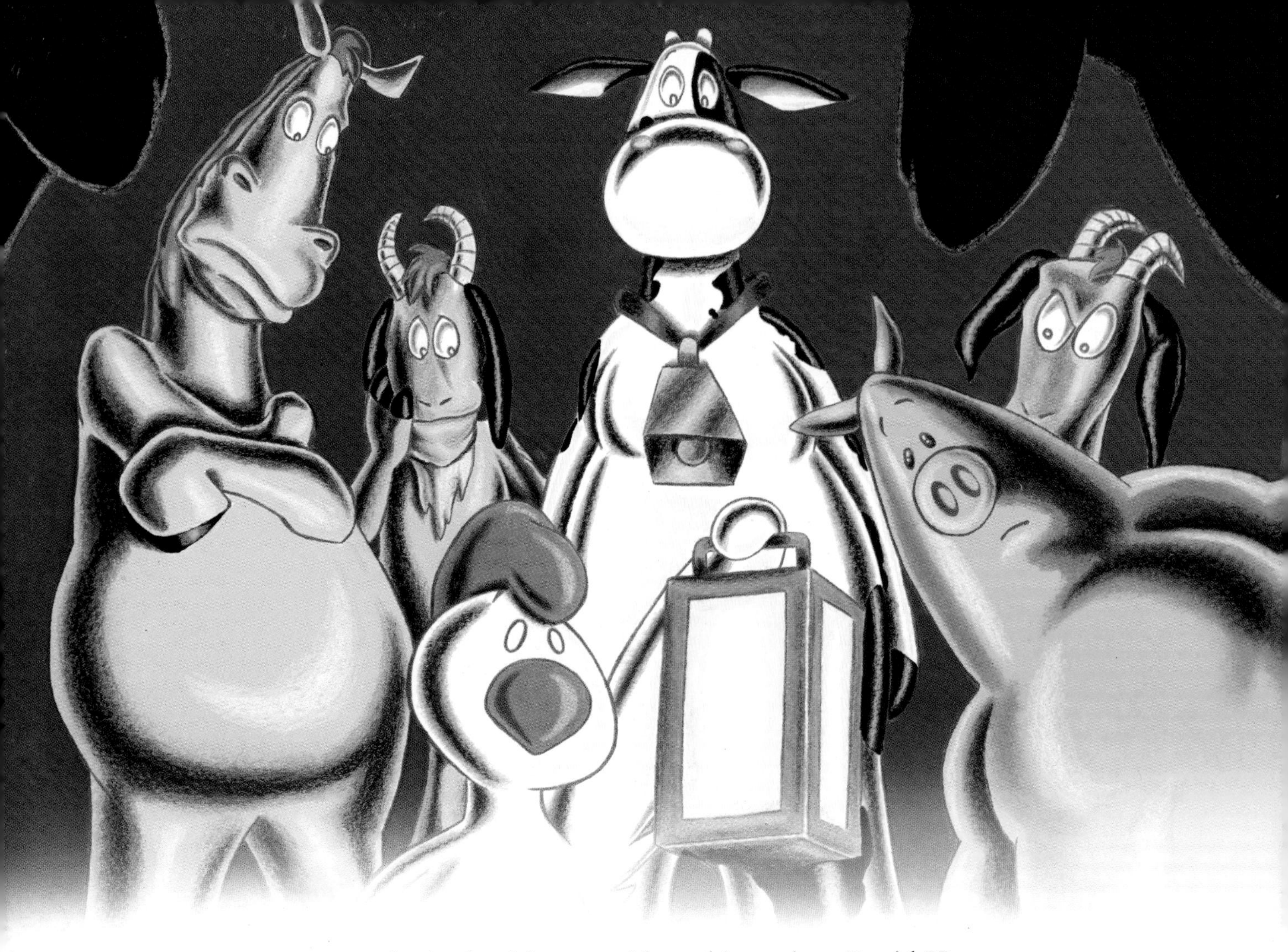

"Somebody should go outside and investigate!" said Horse.
"Yea!" said Chicken. "Here is a lantern!"
"But which one of us should it be?" asked Goat. Everyone was too scared to volunteer.

The animals chose Cow to go out and look around.
"After all," said Pig, "it was Cow who started all of this!"
Cow reluctantly agreed to go. "Shhhhhh . . . " said Cow. "Everybody be very quiet."
She then turned and softly walked out of the big barn door.

SLAM!

SLAM! The other animals loudly slammed the door shut behind Cow! It made an incredible noise!

Cow slowly walked out into the barnyard. Pretty soon the animals looking through the window couldn't see Cow at all.

A loud sound startled Cow. BANG, BANG, BANG! What was that?! BANG, BANG, BANG! Cow was very frightened! Was that a monster?

Cow quickly turned and
pointed her lantern toward
the sound. The
wind was blowing the gate
open and shut! BANG,
BANG, BANG! This was no
monster! Cow was glad it was
only the gate.

FLASH! Everything lit up! The sky and
the farm were suddenly very bright!
So bright that Cow had to shut her eyes!
Was that a monster?

Just as quickly as everything was bright, everything was dark! Cow again couldn't see! What happened? Cow didn't know what to think! Her heart was pounding!

Soon, though, a low rumbling sound filled the air. It was thunder! Cow recognized the thunder and realized that the flash of light must have only been lightning! Cow was glad it was no monster.

Suddenly Cow saw something standing in the shadows watching her.
Cow was very frightened! She took a step toward the dark figure.
"H-h-hello Mr. Monster! Oh, I hope you are a friendly monster!"

Cow moved in a little bit closer. She called out to the monster again. There was still no answer.

Cow was now very close to the dark figure. She continued talking to it, but there was still no answer. "Aren't you going to say anything at all?" asked Cow.

Finally Cow decided to shine her lantern on the figure to get a better look. It wasn't a monster at all! It was just the scarecrow from the field!

The other animals were still looking through the window at the darkness. For a long time they couldn't see anything. Finally, though, they could see the light from Cow's lantern moving toward them. "Here comes Cow!" Goat said.

Cow pushed open the barn door and announced that there were no monsters. She said it was just the wind banging the gate. Everyone was glad to hear the news that they were safe.

Suddenly everyone noticed that
Sheep was still asleep.

Sheep had slept through the
whole thing. As Pig woke her
up, all the animals wanted to know
how she could be so calm
through all of this.
"Weren't you scared like the rest of us?"

Sheep sleepily replied, "God is bigger than anything that might be out in the dark. I may not be the smartest animal on the farm, but I do know that there is nothing to be afraid of. No matter what is in the dark, God is there, too!"

All of the animals were calm now, after listening to Sheep. As the storm got closer, the noises became louder! And as everyone went back to sleep, Cow thanked God for taking care of her.